Anna and Her Grandma
Coping with a Loved Ones Illness

BY LISA SMALLEY

To order additional copies of this book, contact:
Xlibris
844-714-8691
www.Xlibris.com
Orders@Xlibris.com

ISBN: Softcover   978-1-6698-7004-3
         EBook   978-1-6698-7003-6

Library of Congress Control Number: 2023904485

Print information available on the last page

Rev. date: 03/18/2023

I would like to Dedicate this book to my Grandparents,
CB Rodgers and Corene J Rodgers RIH

For as long as Anna could remember, when school was out for the summer, she would always go to her grandma's house. They would always wake up early in the morning and cook breakfast together.

3

Then they would go outside and work in the beautiful vegetable garden Anna's grandma planted every spring.

Anna's grandma made sure she taught Anna how to cook, wash dishes, clean the house, and pick the fresh vegetables out of the garden, just as she did Anna's mom when she was growing up.

Anna would pull out her art set every night to draw pictures for her grandma. She would draw pictures of all the things they did that day, and her grandma would always put them on the refrigerator before she went to bed. Anna loved her grandma so much and didn't like to go to bed at night, so she always wanted to stay up late with her grandma and share girl time. Anna would always end up falling fast asleep on her grandma's lap early, so her grandma would always put Anna in the bed along with a note, saying, "Thank you for our girl time."

The next morning would come, and they would start their normal routine with breakfast, then Anna's grandma would take her to the market to go grocery shopping. They would go down each aisle as Anna's grandma would place the food items in the cart and cross it off her list.

After the shopping was done, Anna could hardly wait because she knew a big treat was coming. Anna and her grandma would always go to the ice-cream store to get ice cream after every shopping trip. This put a big smile on both of their faces.

After Anna and her grandma finished their ice cream, they had to go to the pharmacy so Anna's grandma could pick up her medications. Anna asked her grandma why she had to take her medications, and her grandma told Anna she had to take her medications so she would not forget things.

13

Before she knew it, half of the summer was almost gone. It was almost time for Anna to leave her grandma and go back home with her parents. This was always a sad time for Anna because she loved visiting her grandma during the summertime. She told her grandma she wished she could move back home with her so she could see her every day. Anna's grandma just laughed and said, "Well, baby, if I came to live with you, you wouldn't have a place to visit anymore for the summer, and all of our summertime fun would be over."

"Maybe later on in life," her grandma said, "but for now, let's continue to enjoy our memorable summer together." They both ended the day with a visit to the library, which was a favorite thing for Anna to do. She loved to use her library card to check out a book, read it, and return it the next week.

The next week came, and it was time for Anna to pack her bags up and go back home. After Anna and her grandma prepared their breakfast, there was a knock at the door. When her grandma went to open the door, Anna's mother yelled, "Surprise!"

Anna ran and hugged her mom tight. Her grandma hugged Anna's mom even tighter. The three of them sat down and ate a lovely breakfast together, like they always do at the end of the summer at grandma's house.

Anna's mom helped her mother, who is Anna's grandmother, place all her medications into her pillbox for the entire month so she would not forget to take them.

Anna asked her grandma, "Grandma, when did you last take your medication?"

Her grandma replied, "I took them last night before I gave my bird some water." Her grandma had told Anna she takes her medicine every night before she goes to bed, but Anna never saw her take any.

Anna and her mom packed her bags into the family car and then said their goodbyes to her grandma. Anna blew kisses to her grandma as the family car drove off, and then she yelled out of the window, saying, "I'll see you next summer, Grandma!"

Anna was so excited to tell her mom how much fun she had with her grandma. She talked nonstop to her mom for almost the entire trip home.

When Anna and her mom arrived home, it was time for Anna to take her bath and go to bed because school was starting the next day. Anna was very excited because she could not wait to see her friends and tell them about how she spent another great summer with her grandma during show-and-tell time at school.

All of Anna's friends were excited to hear everything that happened at the house of Anna's grandma over the summer: There was always something new to share with her friends when Anna came back to school.

As the seasons of the year flew by, so did the school year. Before Anna knew it, the summer had rolled around again, and it was time to go back to her grandma's house to spend another wonderful summer. This year   Anna was twelve years old, and her mother allowed her to take the bus down to her grandma's house all by herself instead of her mom taking her.

Anna could not wait 'til her grandma picked her up from the bus station so she could tell her all about her bus ride. After the bus stopped and Anna got all her luggage off the bus, she went to wait for her grandma to pick her up. Anna waited and waited, and she waited, and she waited for her grandma to arrive at the bus station. Her grandma never arrived, so Anna decided to call her grandma on her cell phone. Anna's grandma picked up the cell phone in a panic and asked, "Anna, Anna, where are you? I have been outside waiting for you, and I have not seen you come out. I'm so worried about you. Are you okay?"

Anna said, "Grandma, I'm thinking the same thing about you because I've been standing outside waiting on you for the longest time, and I don't see you anywhere!"

Anna said, "Grandma, what time did you get here to the bus station?"

Anna's grandma said, "Bus station!"

Anna said, "Yes, Grandma, the bus station."

Anna's grandma said, "Baby, I'm so sorry, but I got it mixed up. I am at the airport."

Anna said, "Grandma, it's okay, just take your time and come to the bus station to pick me up."

Finally, her grandma made her way to the bus station to pick up Anna, and they both put Anna's luggage in the trunk of the car.

As Anna's grandma was driving home from the bus station, Anna could tell something was wrong with her grandma, but she just could not figure out what it was. She thought her grandma was tired and just needed to rest.

22

23

When Anna and her grandma got home and unpacked, Anna noticed her grandma's house was a mess. Anna asked her grandma what happened in the house. Anna's grandma said she did some house decorating. Anna had a look of surprise on her face with that answer.

Anna asked her grandma how she was feeling, and her grandma told Anna she was feeling fine but some days, not so fine. Anna looked in her grandma's pill box and noticed her grandma had skipped days taking her pills throughout the entire month.

Anna told her grandma she would help her get her home back in order so it would be much easier for her to find the things she needs. Anna's grandma said, "I would love that because I just can't seem to remember where I put things, and I've been having trouble seeing."

Anna said, "Well, Grandma, let's not worry about it today. Let's go to bed now and we'll start fresh in the morning."

Anna helped her grandma with her bath and changed her into her nightgown. She made sure her grandma took her medicine before she got into bed. Anna noticed her grandma's eyeglasses were hanging on the birdcage in her grandma's room, so she took them off the birdcage and put them on the nightstand next to her grandma's bed.

The next morning Anna got up early to start cooking breakfast for her grandma, now that she was old enough to cook. As she was cooking, Anna started to think of the many times when her grandma used to cook breakfast for her during the summertime visits.

Anna started to notice that things were out of place in her grandma's kitchen. For instance, her grandma had shoes in the refrigerator, magazines in the freezer, and her potted flowers, which she loved so much, in the oven.

Anna was very confused by what she saw. She thought it would be best to deal with the issue later, so she went and got her grandma so they could have their breakfast and talk about her bus trip.

Anna told her grandma all the exciting things about her bus trip, and they laughed together like old times. Then Anna's grandma said, "Well, baby, I have to take a nap now, and I'll get back up and cook breakfast for us, okay?"

Anna said, "But, Grandma, we just ate breakfast."

Her grandma said, "Okay, baby, I'm going to lie down, and I will cook when I get up, okay?" She kissed Anna on the forehead, went back to her room, and lay down to take a nap.

Anna started crying.

She called her mom because she did not know what was going on with her grandma.

Anna told her mom everything that had happened, starting from the bus station and the airport mix-up to everything else that was going on at her grandma's house. Anna's mom said, "Don't worry, I'm on my way."

While on her way to her mother's house, Anna's mom called and made an appointment to get her mom in to see the doctor right away.

Anna's mom arrived late that night. Anna was so happy to see her mom.

Anna's mom hugged Anna and told her she was very proud of her for taking care of her grandma, even though she knew it may have been scary to her. Anna's mom helped Anna process her emotions until she calmed down.

Anna's mom gave her mother a big hug and a kiss on her forehead, and they began to laugh and talk. Anna's mom asked her mom if she was feeling okay, and she said, "No."

Anna's mom said, "Well, Anna and I are going to take you to see your doctor in the morning to make sure that you feel better, okay?"

Her mom just smiled and said, "Okay."

Anna and her mom helped her grandma prepare for bed, and then they went to bed.

The next morning Anna's mom got up very early to cook breakfast for everyone. After everyone ate, she helped her mom get ready for her doctor's appointment. Anna was getting herself ready as well. She just wanted her grandma to be okay.

After they arrived at the doctor's office, they took Anna's grandma and her mom back into a room right away. Anna waited patiently in the waiting room, and she started to think, Wow, this waiting seems just like me waiting at the bus station when Grandma was at the airport. Then she laughed to herself.

All of a sudden, there came a nurse with some papers in her arm. She touched Anna on her shoulder and asked her what her name was.

Anna gave the smiling nurse her name, and the nurse said, "Great! You're the brave young lady that I'm looking for," and asked Anna to follow her.

Anna followed the nurse to one of the educational rooms of the doctor's office. The nurse told Anna how brave she was for taking care of her grandma.

The nurse went on to explain that her grandma was in the middle stages of a memory disease called Alzheimer's/dementia, which is a progressive disease that destroys memory and other important mental functions.

The nurse went on to explain to Anna that it is almost compared to as if someone had fireflies filled in their brain and the fireflies just fly around and light up, then when a person comes down with a disease called Alzheimer's/dementia, some of the fireflies die off and no longer light up in the brain, and the few fireflies that are left in the brain try their hardest to do all the work.

Then the nurse put in a short video to show Anna what happens with fireflies in a brain, just as she described it.

The nurse explained how this disease will cause patients to forget and misplace a lot of things, and they may even go back to acting like a child. Anna's eyes got big as buttons.

Anna told the nurse that was how her grandma was acting, and she didn't know what was going on with her, that's why she called her mom. The nurse told Anna again she was so brave and that she did the right thing to call her mom.

The nurse explained the entire process of the disease to Anna on a level that she could understand it and told Anna that if her grandma would take the new medicine the doctor gives her, it would help some, but the disease would still progress. She told Anna how important it was for the family to take good care of her and give her all the love, hugs, and kisses she could stand. The nurse gave Anna the armful of papers. They were papers about the disease that she could read later.

The smiling nurse asked Anna if she had any questions before she walked her over to her grandma and her mom. Anna said, "No," and thanked the nurse for explaining everything.

The nurse also gave Anna a hotline number to call if she had any questions about Alzheimer's/dementia.

The nurse walked Anna over to the room where her mom and grandma were. Anna just hugged her grandma tight and started to cry. Her grandma said, "Don't cry, baby," as she gently touched Anna's cheeks to dry her tears away.

When they got home, Anna's mom cooked lunch, and then Anna's grandma went to take a nap.

Anna's mom sat Anna down and explained to Anna that Grandma was now going to live with them and they were going to take care of her grandma just like she took care of them.

Anna's eyes lit up like a Christmas tree, and she said, "Mom, you mean that my wish is finally coming true?"

Anna's mom said, "Yes, it is. Your grandma is coming to live with us, and we have to make sure that we take good care of her, okay?"

Anna started dancing and doing her jigs all over the house with excitement because her grandma was coming to live with her, and now the roles have reversed. Her grandma took good care of her when she was young, and now it was time for Anna to help take good care of her grandma.

The next day the movers came and packed up the house of Anna's grandma. They put everything that needed to be in storage in storage; the rest went with her to Anna's house, which was now her new home.

Anna's grandma enjoyed being around her family more. It helped with her memory as well. Anna told her parents that because of what her grandma was going through, she wanted to go to college to become a doctor to help people with their memory.

After that, Anna hugged her grandma and whispered in her ear, "I'm going to change the world."